Is Your Mama A Llama?

Is Your Mama

by DEBORAH GUARIN

Llama?

ctures by STEVEN KELLOGG

SCHOLASTIC INC.

New York Toronto London Auckland Sydney

ISBN 0-590-44725-4

46 45 44   04
                                              40
Printed in the U.S.A.

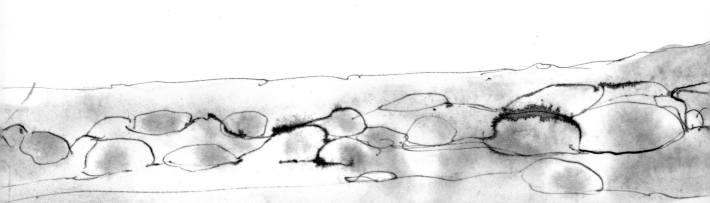

For my son, Joshua,
My Papa and Mama,
My friends Star and Luci . . .
And that one special llama!
— D.G.

Love to
Tatia,
Tremaine,
and to their
marvelous mama.
— Steven Kellogg

"Is your mama a llama?" I asked my friend Dave.

"No, she is not," is the answer Dave gave.

"She hangs by her feet, and she lives in a cave.
I do not believe that's how llamas behave."

"Oh," I said. "You are right about that.
   I think that your mama sounds more like a . . .

"Is your mama a llama?" I asked my friend Fred.

"No, she is not," is what Freddy said.

"She has a long neck and white feathers and wings.
I don't think a llama has all of those things."

"Oh," I said. "You don't need to go on.
I think that your mama must be a . . .

"Swan!"

"Is your mama a llama?" I asked my friend Jane.

"No, she is not," Jane politely explained.

"She grazes on grass, and she likes to say, 'Moo!'
I don't think that is what a llama would do."

"Oh," I said. "I understand, now.
I think that your mama must be a . . .

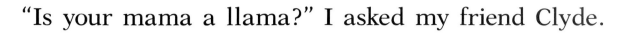

"Is your mama a llama?" I asked my friend Clyde.

"No, she is not," is how Clyde replied.

"She's got flippers and whiskers and eats fish all day . . .
I do not think llamas act quite in that way."

"Oh," I said. "I'm beginning to feel
that your mama must really be a . . .

"Seal!"

"Is your mama a llama?" I asked my friend Rhonda.

"No, she is not," is how Rhonda responded.

"She's got big hind legs and a pocket for me . . .
So I don't think a llama is what she could be."

"Oh," I said. "That is certainly true.
I think that your mama's a . . .

"Kangaroo!"

"Is your mama a llama?" I asked my friend Llyn.

"Oh, Lloyd, don't be silly!" Llyn said with a grin.

"My mama has big ears, long lashes, and fur . . .
And you, of all people, should know about her!"

"Our mamas belong to the same herd, and *you*,
know all about llamas, 'cause you are one, too!"

"Yes, you are right," I said to my friend.
"*My* mama's a . . .

"Llama!"

And this is . . .

THE END